Santa's Big Night first published as *Father Christmas* in Great Britain 2002 by Egmont UK Limited
The Friendly Snowman first published in Great Britain 2002 by Egmont UK Limited
This edition published 2019 by Dean,
an imprint of Egmont UK Limited,
The Yellow Building, 1 Nicholas Road, London, W11 4AN
www.egmont.co.uk

Copyright © 2019 Egmont UK Limited

Santa's Big Night text by Laura Dollin
Santa's Big Night illustrated by Rosalind Beardshaw

The Friendly Snowman text by Catherine Shoolbred
The Friendly Snowman illustrated by Liz Pichon

The moral rights of the authors and illustrators have been asserted.

ISBN 978 0 6035 7575 4
70175/003
Printed in Malaysia

Santa's Big Night

and

The Friendly Snowman

Santa's
Big Night

Father Christmas has a bright, red hat,
Father Christmas has a big, brown sack.

It's Christmas Eve and snowing outside,
The reindeer get ready before their ride.

The clock strikes twelve, and off they go,
Over the roof-tops, through the snow.

When Father Christmas has given his toys
To all the sleeping girls and boys,

He rides back home when it's almost light . . .

. . . And now it's time to say
goodnight!

The Friendly
Snowman

It's cold outside and
the snow is softly falling.

Children build a snowman
out of snow and twigs.

He has a carrot nose, and
his eyes and mouth are buttons.

He wears a woolly hat, with
a matching scarf and mittens.

The children really love him,

he's their favourite winter friend.

And every time they say goodbye,
they're sure they see him wave!